For Fran and [...] in friendship,

Hugh Gilmore

HUGH GILMORE

Scenes From a Bookshop

Short Stories

SoundStars Press
Chestnut Hill, Philadelphia
2012

NOTICE

Scenes from a Bookshop is a work of fiction, and a labor of love, loosely set in the town of Chestnut Hill, Philadelphia, as the author remembers it from the all-too-brief 12 years he operated a used bookshop there from 1995-2007. All characters are fictional and any resemblance to actual persons, living or dead, is purely coincidental.

Hugh Gilmore
Millman Place, Philadelphia
gilmorebookshop@yahoo.com
enemiesofreading.blogspot.com

SoundStars Press
2012
Second printing

Cover design & photo by Hugh Gilmore

ISBN: 1-4751-4804-6
ISBN-13: 9781475148046

DEDICATION

To my mother and father, Loretta & Paul Gilmore

CONTENTS

SCENES FROM A BOOKSHOP is a touching and memorable collection of short stories set in a used & rare book shop in Philadelphia. Brian, the forty-year-old manager gets sent to people's homes to buy books. On one house call he suffers from guilt as he dismantles an old man's library while the man sits and watches him. Back in the shop, he gets a phone call from an abrupt man who's in a hurry to find a book called, *Sexual Astrology*. On another call, a beautiful "Character Actress" involves him in her family drama. Later he meets a charming widow whose husband figures in "Bipolar's what they call it nowadays." In "Chad and Billy Climb to Heaven," he climbs up a broken stepladder into an attic of broken dreams. In "Bags for the Big Bang," a library representing the big bang theory of the universe arrives at the shop in plastic trash bags. In the final story, he's "Trapped in a Bookshop" at night by a maniac who's raiding the Free Books bin outside. And all the while Brian dreams of re-meeting the beautiful "poetry lady" who asked him to find a book for her.

A FASCINATING LOOK BACKSTAGE IN THE WORLD OF OLD BOOKS.

WORKS BY HUGH GILMORE

Local Humor: An Anthology.
With Janet Gilmore, Jim Harris & Mike Todd. 2009.
iUniverse.

Malcolm's Wine: A Noir Crime Novel.
SoundStars Press, 2011

Scenes From A Bookshop: A Short Story Collection.
SoundStars Press. 2012

INTRODUCTION

Be careful what you wish for.

From the very first time I set foot in a bookstore I wanted to own one.

The old bookshops of my youth were magical, mysterious places where the owner himself seemed part of the gray light and dimly lit dusty setting. The books themselves sat on long shelves that seemed to fade into the vanishing point of time itself. The subjects, the titles, the covers, and the dust all added to the romantic idea that I'd stepped away from the loud world of ignorance into a quiet world where the human mind and spirit spoke with unbound eloquence.

The stories that follow are based on images and ideas acquired during the years I ran my shop. Feel free to read them in whatever order you choose. I organized the book according to what I hoped would be a pleasant rhythm for the reader.

While they honor the beauty and lore of old bookshops they also attempt to present a backstage look at what it's like to run one.

Chapter 1
WAITING FOR THE POETRY LADY TO COME BACK

I was out on the sidewalk in front of the shop, sitting on a library kickstool while I cleaned some old books I'd removed earlier that day from the upstairs library of a sad old man. He'd sat in his worn leather armchair only an arm's length away and stared while I removed his lifetime of books from their dusty shelves and boxed them. I could feel his eyes on me as I carried them from the room.

Each time I came back up the creaking staircase for another box was harder—for both of us. I felt sorry for the old man, and also somewhat guilty for being part of the ungentle process that inevitably separates a man from his books.

That's ridiculous, I know. His house was sold; he was moving to a retirement community, and half his mind had marched off without him some time ago. I wanted to resent him for staring at me like I was dismembering his cat, but I knew that, being old and shaky and habit-driven, it was probably his custom to sit in that leather chair, at that hour every day and that I should indulge him his custom while his heart was breaking. (If it was. It's possible he had no idea what was going on and

watching me was no more emotional for him than looking at a fish tank.)

Each book's removal left a clean spot on the dark
wooden shelves, a sharp shadow amidst the light dust, like
something lifted from the snow. That's the most, I wanted
to say to him, we can ask of life, isn't it? But I guessed he
didn't need telling such things. A car horn tooted.

I'd forgotten I was still out on the sidewalk. I looked
up from my reverie. Three cars were caught at the red
light at the corner near the shop, giving the drivers a
chance to watch me flick a dry paintbrush across the top
edge of the book I held, then wipe it with a cotton cloth
and open it to clean the endpapers. I felt like ye olde-time
craftsworker at a Colonial Village theme park. I waved a
small hello to a gray-haired lady whose first reaction was
to startle slightly, as if a portrait had winked at her, but she
waved back and smiled before leaving on the next green
light.

The cordless telephone beside me rang and I picked
it up.

"Hello, Hill Books."

"Yeah, Hill, how you doin'? Yeah, I wanted to ask
you guys...you sell used books, right?" Vying for position.

"All day long."

"Yeah, you do, huh? Okay. Well, this is a out-a-print
book."

A wailing ambulance around the corner made it hard
to hear. Covering my ear with my hand, I said, "What's
the title?" I could barely hear my own voice, the siren's
staccato yelp now riding over the wail, sounding like rapid,
giant drips into a cave pond.

The caller's words were smothered by the noise. It sounded like he said, "Szechuan Estrojalee."

"Hold on," I said, going inside and shutting the door. I switched phone hands for a second so I could honor the O'Toole in the ambulance. ("O'Tooles" are what I call ambulance passengers—after a friend who heart-attacked at 29. When I hear a siren, I tap my knuckles against my heart and cock my chin. It only takes a second.) After I saluted O'Toole, I switched the phone back to my hearing ear again.

"Okay, what was that?" I said. He repeated the title, but just then the wagon itself passed, its diesel engine very loud.

"I'm sorry, an ambulance was going by, what was that title again?"

"*Sexual Astrology.*"

All that for this. WWMD? What Would Malachy, my boss, do?

I chose "Be Kind," from the options flipping through my head, and said, "I'm sorry, we don't have that book. It's too recent for us."

"So you do know that book, though?" Sam Spade lives.

"Is it by 'Martine'"? I said.

Amazing, the things that come back to you. I'd actually seen that book years ago on the night table of a woman while she prepped for me in the bathroom. I'd browsed it while I waited. Martine's prediction came true, happily enough, but only that night and I'd never got another chance to finish that book.

"Yeah, that's the one." Like he was pointing her out in a lineup.

"Well," I said, "that's a recent book and we only sell old books."

Before I could add, "And therefore, goodbye," he jammed in, "Well this is a old book, it's 1976."

Dueling time perspectives—time to terminate.

"Yes," I said, "But we just sell really old books, books published before 1400."

"Oh, I don't think this subject goes back that far." He'd never read the Bible I guessed.

"Maybe Borders has it?"

"They told me to call you."

"They did? Probably just a prank," I said.

"A what?"

"A mistake." I was able to shuttle him over to Triangle Books, whose number he accepted grudgingly before he hung up without saying goodbye or thank you. He sounded desperate, like he needed Martine's prediction immediately. I pictured a pit bear up on two legs, mouth agape, hoping.

I carried the phone outside again and sat down. The reason we clean books outside is that the shop smells dusty and moldy enough without brushing our freshly acquired dirt into it. People often come in and say, "Ah, it even smells like an old book shop in here."

I can't tell by smell anymore, I'm so used to it, though often I see specks hanging in fine suspension near the windows. And I know that whatever we don't breathe eventually settles on every surface. The vacuum cleaner and the air purifier get some of it, but most of the dust and mold stays put. Any particles that leave do so by stowing away in—or on—everyone's lungs, clothes, shoes, hair, face, books, and any other surface suitable for carrying. Some of the dust goes back to the streets, but much of it finds new homes, often in people's libraries.

I picked up another book, Hudson's *Idle Days in Patagonia*, and paintbrushed the top edge. First American edition. 1917. Green cloth, gilt lettering. I open the book. Opposite the title page, a photolith portrait of W.H. Hudson shows him in late middle-age, his hair in a bit of a comb-over above his furrowed brow. He will die five years later. I've tried to do him the honor of removing from his book most of the dust acquired in the old man's library this morning—but there's many a mote remaining if forensics is ever necessary. The old man's remaining dander will be joined with that of the book's next purchaser.

In its own way, the history of the dust and mold on Hudson's book parallels the movement of his words and thoughts from Patagonia to England to America. Like seeds traveling via the sweet, pulpy luggage that is fruit, book mold attaches itself to fine old books in a "whither thou goest" manner. The better the book, the longer its shelf life, the more dust companions it gathers. I closed Hudson's *Idle Days* and put it in the 'cleaned' box.

I was done. I got up and brought everything back inside. Before I closed the door behind me I stepped out and took a final look around and wondered if that pretty woman with the wet hair and sad eyes had driven past today and seen me at my shoeshine stand. And if she did, did she recognize me? Was she tempted to toot?

I started straightening up the shelves, filling gaps, put leaners upright, bracing half-full rows with bookends. I propped a dolphin-shaped bookend against a five-volume set of O. Henry as my thoughts went back to her again.

Usually my flirtations have the life span of a bubble, so I was surprised to find myself thinking about her so much. And that my every thought of her was tinged with hope. She seemed so..."likeable"...was the word that came up. I liked her easy grace. I liked her wit. I very much liked her clear, direct manner. And deeper—this was where I'd been hooked—that little glimpse of sadness in her eyes made it seem she needed to be loved, needed a friend. I wanted and needed to be that someone.

I went over to the computer to check the shipping status of the book I'd ordered for her. I tapped a few keys and there it was: the folks in Ohio said they'd shipped it yesterday via Media Mail. It would arrive in three to ten days. That news perked me up for the rest of the afternoon.

No customers came in the shop that day. Neither did Malachy, who usually came over at least to count the till. At five o'clock I locked up and left. Going home, for me, means walking twenty steps down the alley next to the shop, unlocking the door, and going up eighteen steps to my apartment. My hair was dry and stiff with dust, and my skin begged for a shower.

Later, I sat by the window with a glass of wine, watching it get dark outside, noticing the hospital lights' pretty green glow against the faded blue of the evening. Another O'Toole went wailing by and as the sound faded I thought about how glad I was that I had the poetry book's arrival to look forward to. That the sad-eyed lady—her name was Canace—might come into my life helped balance the image of the man whose books I'd plundered today, the old man whose dust I'd so willingly washed from my hair tonight.

Chapter 2
BAGS FOR THE BIG BANG

About eleven o'clock the next morning, Sam the postman stepped partly through the doorway, just enough to extend his arm to the counter and drop a package. "Here ya go. Just what you always wanted—another book."

Before I could ask where the package was from he'd closed the door and was gone.

I looked at the shipping label. Mansfield, Ohio. Had to be the book of poetry I'd ordered for Canace (I was charmed that her parents had named her after Canacee of *The Faerie Queene*), the sad-eyed lady I couldn't stop thinking about. Now I'd have an excuse to call the number she'd given me, "in case I find a copy." Originally I'd told her we don't do book searches. She looked so disappointed as she left, I ordered the book later on my own, partly to be nice, mostly as an excuse to talk to her again. She'd left a phone number in case I found a copy.

As I started to tear the unzip tab on the box, I got an uneasy feeling that my boss, Malachy, might step in and "catch" me. He'd want to know about the package. He'd made it quite clear he didn't want my time wasted ordering books from the Internet for walk-in customers.

"Tell them go to Triangle for that kind of thing. We're a book shop." I'd tried to tell him several times that the basic difference between ordering from a catalog, his preferred—and almost sacred—method, and ordering from the Internet was that the Internet was faster. But he'd never learned to use a computer and he wasn't about to start now. He'd wonder why I'd ordered a book without asking him in advance. And his eyebrows would fly up into his scalp if I told him it was for a lady.

About a half-dozen times during the years I'd worked for him I dated women I'd met in the shop. I could tell by his stiffness that he minded, but he managed not to say anything to me until the time a breakup spilled over into the shop. Then he put his foot down. What happened in the shop was his business and he didn't have to tolerate "monkeyshines." In his dependably strict manner he told me I'd better cut it out, or I could look elsewhere for a job.

Now, standing there holding the package, I wanted to avoid repeating that scene. I had paid for this online book using my own credit card, but I'd ordered it on company time. And I knew I couldn't explain my innocent diversion without feeling guilty under his stare. I didn't want to cheapen myself by lying. I walked outside and down the alley to my car, which I park out back, and put the package under the passenger seat. I guess I should have had the package sent to my apartment, but I wasn't thinking clearly when I ordered the book. Poetry will do that to a man if a woman's his motive.

I wasn't back at the desk ten minutes when Malachy came struggling through the door sideways, carrying an overfilled Hefty Steel Sack garbage bag over his shoulder. I hurried over to help him, but he kept going, just murmuring, "More outside" as he passed. Three more large bags were across the street on the sidewalk. I ran over and grabbed one and was surprised by the weight of it. I needed to lift and swing it to get it over my shoulder and its sudden weight almost pulled me backwards when I felt its force.

Two more trips and all four bags were in the back of the shop. Malachy had already started shelving the books from the first bag onto our new-acquisitions case.

He'd just come from what we call a "house call" to purchase some books. As I helped him he told me about the lady he'd bought them from. She'd told him that one night last year she'd been sitting with her husband in the living room, both of them reading and enjoying a glass of wine, having a normal evening at home, when her husband stood up to go get a refill, but remained standing by his chair for a few seconds before he said, "I don't feel right," and sat down again. He died of a stroke within minutes. Only forty-six, he was. It took a year for her nerves to settle. Now she was moving to another state and taking with her as little of her physical past as possible. She told Malachy that if he wanted even one book he had to buy them all. Most of them were good books, so he bought the lot, about nine hundred books.

Well, why did he bring four bags of them back to the shop with him? Normally, he would pay for the books, return to the shop, and send me to go pack and carry them.

He told me that after he and the widow agreed on a purchase price and he wrote the check, the woman said she had to leave immediately to take her dog to the veterinarian. If the boss wanted to send his assistant back to the house, that was all right, she said, because the painters and plasterers would be here any minute and they had a key and would let me in.

Oh no, no, no, no, Malachy thought. He distrusts anyone left alone with books he's paid for, especially antique-looking books that might fit in a person's pocket. Books like that tend to walk away unless carefully watched. Every bookman and antiques dealer has had repairmen try to sell them old things they'd "found," or things "left" in an old house they were working on. They're not the only danger, either. Uncles, cousins, long-lost brothers, nephews, nieces, friends, neighbors and other opportunists will also pilfer from a bookman's unattended stack, probably believing that one or two books would never be missed. Which isn't true, especially with an experienced bookman like Malachy. Better safe than sorry, he says.

He decided to get the best books out of the house before the workmen arrived, but he hadn't any boxes with him since he'd walked from his home to the house call, which was a mile from the shop. He asked the lady if she had some plastic garbage sacks, or leaf bags, which she did. He then removed the most valuable books from the book cases, a number that filled four sacks, and left, just as the painters arrived. He carried the four bags onto the porch, then down across the long driveway and out to the street, one by one. Then he'd carried the first bag a full block, put it down, and walked back for the second bag. Then the third, then the fourth, and, proceeding a block at a time in that manner, he transported all four bags the mile to our shop, walking at last four miles in total carrying bags that must have weighed about fifty pounds each, not to mention the books' corners making sharp bulges that dug into his back as he humped them to their new home. He was rubbing and stretching out his shoulders the whole time he told me this story.

We had unloaded the sacks and put all the books onto the holding shelves when Malachy decided to play one of his educational games with me. He pointed to the books as an aggregate and asked me what I could tell about their previous owner. He loves giving me these little tests and I love taking them, so I looked the books over carefully. Nearly all were leather-bound, mostly early nineteenth century, with a smattering of eighteenth and seventeenth. I considered the titles, authors and subjects for a while and said I saw no pattern to them.

"Right," he said in the way that says you're correct, but haven't yet arrived at the deeper truth. "So what does that tell you?" he said.

I said it told me that, first of all, the man was not a "collector." With no similarity of subject, theme, or author, their only common feature was that they were old and leather-bound. Also, the bindings were not distinctive enough to make me think it was a binding collection.

"And so?" he asked. I ventured that they'd simply been bought by one person who acquired any old book that tickled his fancy when he saw it for sale, primarily because he liked the charm of age.

"Good guess," he said, "but short of the mark."

He reminded me that people charmed by the age of books are usually cheap. They buy odd volumes of *The Spectator*, for example, or Washington Irving, or Watts' sermons.

The books we were guessing about were too tasteful and expensive for a buyer like that. What we were looking at, he said, was probably a small sample from a collection that had been inherited through several generations. He said it was like the Big Bang that started the universe.

A man gathers individual books about his subject one by one from many sources and gradually forms a collection in the truest sense. But if he dies, and has made no plans for what happens next, the books get passed along to his heirs and friends, usually in small groups because the inheritors lack both the space to store a great library and the taste to appreciate what made it great.

As an ancestor's family grows larger and more dispersed, so do the books. Uncle Henry, would you like Grandfather's sailing books? Cousin Charles, do you think your daughter would like these books about dogs? Within a few generations, the books become mixed into a modern dust-jacketed library in the puzzling manner of shrapnel in an old tree that lines a field where once a battle took place, their presence decipherable only to people who think archeologically, like the boss.

Too bad the books had come from an exploded collection, I thought. Collections are much more interesting than aggregations. Large, thematic, systematically-built collections are an accomplishment worthy of a lifetime's endeavors. Anything else, the boss sniffed, "is just an accumulation of souvenirs." I shriveled at the thought of my own library—a mere accretion.

Malachy told me to take the van and go back for the rest of the books, the "meatloaf," as he puts it, the filet mignon having already arrived in plastic leaf sacks.

There were another eight hundred books, including five shelves of oversized art books, he said. My rule of thumb is twenty-five regular books or ten big art books per box, so I went to our storage room and pulled down, including some extras, fifty flattened, reusable boxes. I put them in the van and left.

On my way over I suddenly thought about the package for Canace and how it was now sitting under the passenger seat of my car. What if she'd left the store the other day, went directly to Triangle Books, and found a copy of the book she'd wanted? The pang of disappointment I felt at that thought surprised me. I hardly knew this woman, yet that sharp little stab of feared loss told me I liked her more than I knew. I was hooked a little. I'd grown accustomed to being alone and yet a small obstacle between me and a mere pleasantry made me feel slightly bereft. Another day's delay won't make such a difference, I told myself. I'll call her anyway and find a way to keep her speaking on the phone.

At the book house, unfortunately, I couldn't park the van any closer than fifty feet from the back door. The hauling of this library would take longer and be harder than I thought.

After one of the painters let me in, there was more bad news. Most of the books were on the second and third floors. It took three hours of packing, handcarting, and loading to get the books from the house into the van. And the reverse again when I returned to the shop.

Malachy looked up from typing book descriptions long enough to ask if everything went all right. I said yes, and he lowered his periscope and went back under.

It took me an hour to haul the books to the back room. Malachy pecked away at his catalogue cards in the meantime, the keys of his old Royal clacking out the monotonous rhythm of a life spent selling books.

The rest of the afternoon, I kept busy to make the time pass more quickly. I unpacked the books we'd bought today, sorted and cleaned them, and priced some of the ones that looked as though they'd have better-than-average values. All the while, I stayed conscious of the book lady, thinking of what I might say when I called her from my apartment, one way or the other.

At closing time Malachy was still busily typing catalog cards. Something was up, but I couldn't imagine what. When I finished bringing in our sidewalk sale table books, I flipped the "Closed" sign and looked over at him.

He said, "Brian, before you leave, I wonder if you have time to talk a bit?"

"Yeah, sure," I said.

"Good," he said, "why don't we sit over here?" He went behind the desk and nodded at the other chair for me to sit.

Someone outside rattled the door handle a few times, ignoring the two "Closed" signs on the doors' windows. We waited for him to give up, which took another minute.

When he did, Malachy said, "I've had something to tell you all day, but I didn't want to be interrupted by shop business."

I nodded.

"My daughter Elizabeth's husband Carl died yesterday. Last night. I'm flying out to Minnesota tonight to be with her as soon as I can."

He picked up a woven homemade bookmark I'd removed from a book this morning and left it on the desk. He stroked his thumb across it while he went on talking. "Carl had left work and was crossing the street to get to the parking lot when a hit-and-run driver ran him down." He tightened his lips and turned down the corners of his mouth at the end of each sentence.

He put the bookmark down. Witnesses said the driver was an old man who could barely see over the steering wheel. He never looked back, or hesitated, just kept on driving. Someone got his license number and gave it to the police. Carl died on the way to the hospital in the back of the emergency wagon, though the EMTs worked on him through the whole run.

The news sickened me.

"Elizabeth needs my help," Malachy said. "I'll be out there for a while. At least two weeks."

He told me what he expected of me, how he hoped I'd keep his shop hours unless something unavoidably drew me away. He said if I had to choose between making a great house call and keeping the shop open, I should go on the call. "Good books are harder to buy than sell," he reminded me. He would leave twenty pre-signed checks for me, if I had the chance to do some buying. I was to consult with him on any payments over a thousand dollars. Stay in touch. Answer the phone. Put the mail aside. And so on.

I assured him that I'd take care of everything. This wouldn't be the first time I covered when he was away. Not to worry about things on this end. I felt sorry for him. He loved his daughter and his grandchildren and I could see, even through the impassivity of his face, that the thought of their suffering was painful for him.

He started to stand up, I guessed to leave, but sat down again. He said, "I suppose I should put off saying this until I return, but I feel obligated to tell you this."

I felt nervous. Was this going to be about the book I ordered?

He said, "Elizabeth and Carl weren't getting along before this happened. They were considering a separation. I never thought I'd be telling you this, because it's personal information, but I need to, so you don't think this is a sudden decision on my part. Elizabeth has lupus. Do you know what that is?"

"Yes," I said, "it's awful."

"Yes, awful."

He was quiet for a moment. Then he went on, "With Carl gone, she needs my help. I've decided to move out there and be what help I can."

The question of what he'd do with the shop hovered between us.

"If you can afford to buy my business, I'll sell it to you. I think you know enough now to make a living from it."

I didn't say anything, just nodded. I was thinking, "Oh my. Oh my." I felt, despite the pain and tragedy Malachy had just described, maybe even because of it, as though I'd finally been recognized as worthy by someone older, wiser, someone who'd found me worth mentoring and was now placing his confidence in me–something I'd often regretted had never happened to me. Despite the solemnity of his manner and the reasons for his telling me this news, I was touched. Frightened, also, by the weight of what I'd been offered, but touched deeply.

He said, "I think you'd make a good bookseller. But I need to make something very clear to you."

"Yes," I said.

"I don't know what your financial status is, and it's none of my business. But I have to tell you this. I haven't set the price for selling my business yet. When I do, however, I'm telling you plainly, the price will not be set with anything in mind but fair value. I will set a fair price and I will not deviate from it one penny because of your situation. I'll be flexible on terms, but the price will be set without any consideration of what you can or cannot afford."

I wanted to thank him or assure him that I understood, but everything that came to mind sounded glib. I nodded a few times and then told him, "I'm sorry about Carl, and Elizabeth."

"Yes," he said. And we parted.

Partly dragged down, partly happy and energized, partly in a panic, I went back to my apartment over the shop. I was hungry, but couldn't eat. I was tired, but sat staring out the window at the the smokestacks of the hospital up the street. I wondered how much the shop might be worth. Would the bank lend me enough to get a mortgage?

And I'd shift in my chair by the window and hear an ambulance siren go by again. Poor Carl, coming out of work, not knowing he'd get hit by a car. And the old man who hit him...what must that have been like...having police knock at your door for something you had no knowledge you were guilty of doing? And then I'd drift back to wondering how much money I'd need to raise or borrow to buy the shop. What would it be like to be my own boss?

I remembered the package that I'd hidden in my car and went downstairs to retrieve it. Back upstairs again, I sat at my kitchen table and opened it. *The Pocket Book of Verse: Great English and American Poems.* "249 poems by 77 of the world's greatest poets." 16th printing, March, 1943. Simple enough. It shouldn't be so scarce, you would think. There'd been only three copies available for sale on the Internet. I drifted into reading the introduction.

I got no further than opening randomly to page vii of the introduction and reading Wordsworth's definition of poetry as "the spontaneous overflow of powerful feelings recollected in tranquility." I'd certainly had my share of powerful feelings in the past few days, but recollected tranquility was going to be on hold till I'd talked to the lady I'd bought this book for.

The book of poems was in my hand, but its poetry was not in my heart yet. I was quite conscious, as I picked up the telephone, that, whether she answered or not, I might never know tranquility again.

Chapter 3
CHARACTER ACTRESS

A woman named Jeanne called. She had a nice speaking voice, but her tone was sharp and impatient. She frequently interrupted me. I thought she was rude in the way some rich people can be when they're talking to "tradesmen," but as she went on I sensed she was simply frazzled. And I also noticed as she went on talking that her classy diction was an overlay, that she'd learned to speak well after having grown up speaking like the rest of us Philadelphians. She was telling me she needed someone to come look at her parents' books.

I'm sure I didn't help her mood by being unenthusiastic about the books she described, but she herself disparaged them as she read from her notes: Sets of Victor Hugo, in cloth, with paper labels. "Great Stories from Great Writers." Things like that. I began looking for a polite way to tell her I wasn't interested.

The situation we were in is like a contest. The caller wants someone to remove all the books from the house and pay a lot of money for them, believing bottom line that since all books contain wisdom, they all are valuable.

Booksellers will pay well for good books, but don't want to waste time chasing after unsaleable books. So, it's important to ask enough questions to get a sense of what the caller's books are like. Often they'll lie or exaggerate about the books, or, describe them in a deliberately vague way they hope will force you to come see for yourself. If that fails, they'll tell you they don't want any money, they just need to get rid of them.

In theory, making the books free seems like it would be a trade-off for the bookman, the idea being that he should be able to salvage enough to make the whole deal profitable. That is not only not true, it is a trap that leads novice booksellers to accumulate vast amounts of books that will never sell.

However, if the caller lives near the shop, we'll usually drive over just to keep our rivals out of our neighborhood. Besides, the lady (despite being annoying) seemed pretty desperate and something beneath her words touched me. I agreed to come over. It doesn't cost anything but time to look around and give advice. And besides, you never can tell. People usually tell you over the phone only about the books they think are special, sometimes while using a less attractive, but valuable, book as a lamp support. The lady's name was Jeanne Marie Egan.

The address was in a modest Mt. Airy neighborhood. Though they were row houses, they were made of fieldstone—an income notch or two above the usual Philadelphia red brick. One of the finest collections of Western Americana I've ever bought came out of such a row house and one of the most dismal libraries I've ever seen was housed in a private home designed by an internationally famous architect. So, I'm fairly open-minded when I'm given an address, though I must say that rich people usually have more valuable books than the rest of us.

Jeanne Marie said there'd be a dumpster out front, but they wouldn't throw any books in there until I'd had a chance to examine them. Not an encouraging image, but I committed myself, so that was it.

Dumpsters on site are an obvious sign that the house has a lot of junk in it—either things that were junky to begin with, or things that became junky through neglect: leaking roofs, mold, animals allowed to eliminate indoors (e.g. what we later called the "doo-doo–pee-pee house," where six uncaged birds and two small unwalked dogs had the run of the house, which was a smelly, awful, fouled mess...but half the books were rare. Malachy had me buy them and take all but one immediately to an up-country auction. That one was a first edition of the Brothers Grimm in English.)

Jeanne Marie said she and her brother would be there all day Saturday. I said I couldn't come on Saturday, because the shop is open, but would come first thing Monday. She returned to her original exasperated tone of voice in agreeing to Monday. That bothered me since I felt I was doing *her* a favor, convinced as I was that nothing was in it for me other than feeling that I'd given an obviously depressed and anxious person some emotional relief.

Except I changed my mind about Saturday and screwed up.

I woke up early that morning, still feeling tired, and started to console myself with the thought that I had Monday off, but then remembered the Mt. Airy job. Jeanne Marie had said she'd be there all day Saturday, so I decided to get my walk-through over with before I opened the shop. That way I'd still have Monday free.

Nothing's ever simple though. When I drove to the house I saw that a couple of chairs and wooden boxes had been set in the street to claim the parking spaces...probably for the dumpster. The storm door of the house was closed but the inside door open, which I took as a sign that Jeanne Marie and her brothers were hard at work. They'd be as glad to get this over with as I would.

I knocked. No lights were on inside. I knocked again, louder, thinking they must be working upstairs. Out of the gloom an old woman in a faded turquoise bathrobe appeared at the door. Her hair was a dark, reddish brown, too young for her heavily creased face, and she looked tired, really tired, a person caught near the end of an endurance contest. The voice on the phone and the age of this woman didn't match, but that's an easy mistake to make.

"Hello, Jeanne Marie, I'm Brian the bookman. I had some extra time this morning, so I hope you don't mind that I'm here now.

"Jeanne Marie isn't here yet," she said, stepping back into the dimly lit living room, holding the door open for me to come in.

I stepped in. A reading chair with a standing lamp beside it and an ottoman in front, were in the center of the living room. Surrounding them at the edges of the room were packed boxes and piles of things ready for packing.

"Who's down there?" said an angry, whispery voice from upstairs.

She ignored the voice.

"I'm sorry," she said, "I can't help you. I don't know how they want to do it, or where anything is."

A coach's whistle blew shrilly upstairs.

Nodding upwards she said, apologetically, "Jim has Alzheimer's and I've got to take care of him."

"Oh, yes, well, that's okay...Is Jeanne Marie your daughter?"

"Yes, but she's not here and I can't help you. I'm sorry."

She spoke in the tone used by people speaking to an official they think is about to cite them or arrest them, or foreclose the mortgage. I wanted to reassure her, but didn't know what to say.

I looked back at her and saw she now stood with her mouth open, tears ready to roll out of her eyes, a sight made worse by her child-like compliance.

"I'll come back when Jeanne Marie's here," I said, backing out the door, sorry for having upset her. She began apologizing to me. I said, "No, I'm sorry. I should have called first." But she apologized again, which I felt I needed to apologize for provoking from her. Thus it went until I was able to go down the steps and walk back to my car, feeling stupid and clumsy for having upset her.

I hadn't asked, but I had the impression from Jeanne Marie that her parents were dead and gone, or at least gone, so I'd not anticipated finding them there. My knocking on their door so early had confused people who were already upset—not so much by moving, as from being moved.

And if I didn't feel bad enough already as I drove away, I knew that I did not want to return on Monday, my day off. Nothing about the furnishings in the house suggested that there would be rare or collectible books there. And Jeanne Marie's mother—I'd seen her before. I wasn't sure where, but it was associated with thrift shops or yard sales. Bargain hunting. In fact I thought I remembered her as a semi-regular browser of the "Free" box of books we always leave on the shop's doorstep.

That afternoon Jeanne Marie called me at the shop. She sounded a little annoyed that I'd upset her mother, but from her tone I extracted the idea that she was used to her mother being upset and also that she didn't have time to waste on upsets or anger, there was too much to be done, too little time to do it, so let's cut to the chase, Was I coming Monday or not? Yes? Good. See you then. Hang up. She'd decided my role in this family drama before I could resign from the audition.

I awoke early on Monday and drove back to Mt. Airy. The small dumpster in front the house was overflowing. I saw an old steamer trunk, string-wrapped piles of moldy old books, lumber, lamp poles, wooden boxes, mop handles, wine racks, cardboard boxes, coat hangers, kitchen bags, and more. No lights were on in the house. Both front doors were closed.

I knocked on the storm door. Ten seconds, no answer. I opened the storm door and knocked on the glass pane at the top of the wooden door. No answer. Rang both the door buzzers, (why two?) though I was sure the buzzers had stopped working long ago.

I started back to the car but a small red pick-up truck whizzed up the street and stopped in front of the house where I stood. A woman got out and said "Hi, I'm Jeanne Marie." She began rampaging her purse, fussing out loud, looking for a key in the sort of frantic way that hinders a search.

I watched and waited. And looked. Anne Marie was well-packaged. A bit worn, but a woman with the sort of good looks that could make Philip Marlowe fall down a manhole on his way over to light her cigarette. About forty, blonde, lightly creased, carrying a porous Irish complexion and tight blue jeans you'd want to watch doing the Texas two-step. All in all, the kind of harsh attractiveness that makes you want to hide your heart out back somewhere before you step in and introduce yourself. I forget what she was wearing up top.

I mention these details only because the bookseller's life is normally a dull one. We live in a gray world, where gray-haired people inhabit dim rooms filled with dust-covered books. We seldom deal with good-looking women wearing ultra-tight jeans who say, "Follow me," as they begin to ascend a staircase, which I needed to do twice in order to get to the third floor.

But not before pausing momentarily in the living room after her mother opened the door.

"Mom you remember Mister Gilmore. He was here Saturday. We're going to go up and look at the books. You have to take Dad to the doctor's this morning don't you?"

"He won't go."

"What. What do you mean 'He won't go'?"

"He won't go."

"Okay, I'll take care of this."

We went up the worn, green-carpeted stairs. At the top, she said, "I can't wait till this is all over with."

"It's a lot of work, I know," I said.

"Oh you can't believe it. My brothers and I did nothing all day on Saturday but throw stuff out. You saw the dumpster. It's filled already. I should have got the big one."

"Amazing how much stuff accumulates."

"I gotta get back to my life. My family, my work, everything. I'm over here constantly. Let's go up to the third floor and start there."

In the dark hallway I could see four bedrooms, one with its door mostly shut. As she walked past it, she shouted through the crack, "You've got to get up. Get dressed. You have to go to the doctor's this morning."

"I do?"

"Yes you do. Get up. Get going."

We went upstairs, she talking to me the whole time about how many loose ends she was taking care of and how stressful the situation was. That was easy to see. We went into a bedroom, and she pointed to a bookcase. I went over. Nearly all the books were her brothers' old school texts and paperbacks. Not for me, thank you. The low optimism I'd started with dipped further.

Though I wanted to leave then, manners of the useless kind made me stay on and play through the rest of the ordeal. I've been in this situation before. This is where I simply turn off the meter and attend to the story happening around me. It's like slipping through the plasma screen into a television show happening around you. "The story of the day the bookseller came, and what he did while he was here, and how he spoke about us and our books." A story to be told ages and ages hence.

"Nothing here, huh?" she said.

"Mostly school books."

"Can't anybody use them?"

"Not really. They change the editions all the time."

"Yeah, I didn't think so. Well, I wasn't sure, so we're checking it out right? There's more downstairs."

As we passed her father's door on the second floor she said, "Excuse me a minute." And opened the door enough to look in. "You getting ready? Oh god. Hold on a minute."

She ushered me into one of the other side rooms. "I think they put the books all in here. These boxes, I think. Yeah. Here. Can you look in these?"

She went out, I assumed to her father's room. I got on all fours and started looking through the boxes; there were six of them, on the carpet of the otherwise-empty room. More textbooks and Signet Classics paperbacks with passages highlighted. Some coffee table books about jet planes, a few hardbacks on subjects like the Hopi Indians, panzer divisions, *The Greening of America*, *Siddhartha*. Books we see often. Nothing we could use for resale back at the shop.

When I finished the fourth box I stood up. Jeanne Marie came back in, leaving the door open, and began talking to me while simultaneously monitoring the hall behind her.

"What about that box there," she said.

I opened the criss-crossed flaps. Some Philadelphia books with neighborhood pictures were on top. I'm hopeful. If nothing else I can always use local history. They always sell. Perhaps there are more. Perhaps this is the one box that will make the visit worthwhile. Down on my knees once more, I begin rummaging again when my peripheral vision senses a blur appear and pause in the doorway.

I don't look up. I know who's there and that this is a potentially awkward moment. Just as you can sense what kind of animal is in a cage at the zoo by looking at the faces of the people watching the animal, his family's behavior led me to suspect that the old man who'd emerged from his closed, dark bedroom door to pause and look at me on the floor of the adjoining room was either deranged or badly confused and I didn't want to add to his confusion, or possible rage, by seeming to be anything other than a painted figure kneeling over an opened cardboard box. A *tableaux vivant* of THE ETERNAL BOOKSELLER. I froze mid-frame, as it were, a portrait of concentration, trying to look as philosophical as Erasmus himself while I waited for the old man and the moment to pass.

"Who's that?" I heard him whisper.

"He's just here looking at some things," his daughter said. Smart answer. Vague. Open to lots of interpretations, most of which would probably require too much energy for a confused old man to follow-up on.

In such situations I try to keep quite, especially with a formidable daughter present. "He may be an old ornery bastard, but he's OUR ornery old bastard, so don't patronize him." A lot to think about, crouched over a box of books in an abandoned room, especially a box of what turned out to be unsellable books.

Fortunately, he moved on. Unfortunately, though, he went back into his bedroom. She went after him and said firmly through the closed door. "You have to get ready for the doctor's." Then she returned to ask me, "So there's nothing you want, huh? What do you think I should do with this stuff? I know what I'm going to do. There's a guy who will take it all out of here. And pay some money too. All in one fell swoop."

"Might be a good idea," I said. "It's a lot simpler that way."

"Wait a minute," she said, and half-closed the door, looking out into the hallway and obviously watching her father, Jim, go by. "Oh God," she said nearly gasping and came into the room with me, closing the door further so I couldn't see. "It's so embarrassing," she muttered, almost in teenager fashion. I heard the bathroom door close and water start humming in the wall pipes between the bathroom and us.

I stood up again. She indicated with gestures that we should wait a minute until the coast was clear.

With nothing better to say, out of curiosity, I said, "You said before that you were neglecting your work," (She'd said 'neglecting my work,' rather than "job,' before, so I thought her answer might be interesting. "What kind of work do you do, do you own a business?"

"Oh, my husband and I own a construction company. Strictly small jobs. We've built some Burger Kings, some apartments, things like that."

Packed into her tight jeans, the long hair, her take-charge manner, I could see that. Could see her married to a guy named 'Rock," or something like that. A stud kind of guy. Coming out to the construction site and making all the carpenters drop their nail-guns.

"And I act, too, so I'm always running up to New York."

I liked that expression; "I act." A verb, rather than "I'm an actress." She clarified the distinction in the same breath. "I do character acting. Strictly characters, voice-overs, things like that. Nothing dramatic. I don't do drama."

Well, like any red-blooded American boy, I would have loved to spend the rest of the morning standing in a dim, sad room of worthless boxes of used books and magazines, arm's-length from a stacked actress in tight jeans framed against the doorway, her Alzheimer-stricken father making the water pipes hum while her worn-out mother fretted downstairs, but before I could ask another question and capitalize on knowing a New York character actress so well, a thump from the bathroom broke the spell.

She hurried out to the bathroom and while I half-overheard the muffled voices from there, I thought about what she'd said. A character actress. Nothing dramatic, no, because she wasn't saying words someone else had written to be performed for an audience bigger than the one assembled in that small row house on a busy Saturday morning. Me, the ticket man walking down the aisle, a young woman riding the middle, and two old people back in the caboose.

I gathered up the three Philadelphia picture books and a "History of the Friendly Sons of Saint Patrick in Philadelphia" and when the woman who played the character actress came out of the bathroom, I played The Bookman and said, "This is all I can use. I'm sorry. I'll give your mother twenty dollars." The daughter lady acted glad for that and for the overall appraisal and said she now knew better what she should do.

I sat by the window that evening remembering Jeanne Marie and her parents as though the visit I'd made had been a stage show I'd seen:

She and the bookseller walk past the steamy bathroom where the guy who plays the old Alzheimer patient is half-singing, half humming "For Me and My Gal," and then they playfully descend the stairs. In the dimmed living room, a pole lamp illuminates the only chair. In it, a small woman, made up to look old and tired, but nonetheless spritely, sits with a mug of coffee in one hand, a pastry in the other. Mother and daughter argue briefly about who should keep the twenty-dollar bill.

The bookman pauses in the doorway, turns his head to accept the daughter's embarrassingly warm (and enjoyed) kiss on his cheek, and then he steps out onto the stone porch. He takes a small breath and exits stage left carrying his hard-won books.

After that, if the show runs long enough, and as the audience has already guessed, the bookman eventually goes upstairs and puts on that gray bathrobe. He's a natural to play that role.

Chapter 4
BIPOLAR'S WHAT THEY CALL IT NOWADAYS

On Friday morning I had to go on a call to a widow's house in nearby Roxborough, a side-street row house that had no parking out front. I circled the block and found the alley that ran behind the houses and bounced slowly through its potholes looking for house numbers. There were none, but I had remembered him describing the house as the fourth from the corner, so I parked under a mulberry tree and went in the fourth gate. On the backyard clothesline hung a blue, flowered, old-fashioned housedress, a bra, and panties, all small. I hoped I wasn't embarrassing her by walking past them.

Mrs. McBreen was not small. Medium sized plump, I'd say, and was surprised, but didn't seem embarrassed that I'd come to the back door. I apologized, for form's sake, and we walked through the narrow kitchen, dining room, and living room to the front room. It was ten in the morning, but with light coming in only through jalousie-covered windows in the front and rear, the interior was dim. True to widow practice among this Greatest Generation, not a single light bulb was lit. They survived the Great Depression, World War II, Korea, and Vietnam, and they don't need to be sitting around in the daytime with the lights on. I see it all the time. In my early years in this business I tried a few times to explain Seasonal Affective Disorder and the need for plenty of light to keep your spirits from sinking, but I'd always hear the cost/benefit wheels clicking in their heads just before they told me "Oh, I couldn't waste electricity like that."

She showed me the cherry wood bookcases that occupied an entire wall of the sunroom. Home made, but well-done, filled with books, some whatnots in front of them, a few framed pictures. A glance was enough. I told her that the books were more modern than what we usually "can use for our customers," but if she didn't mind, I'd go ahead and dig in, maybe "find a treasure."

Nice books. Good taste. Readers. Book lovers. But no treasures. Among the children's books, some Tasha Tudors and Arthur Rackhams, but third and fourth editions. Good fiction, of the "literature" kind: *Tom Sawyer, The Razor's Edge*, Dickens, and so on. No Best Seller blockbusters like Maeve Binchey, Tom Clancy, Faye Kellerman, Particia Cornwell, Mary Higgins Clark. A few Thomas Merton titles. Caribbean travel guides from the Seventies.

Pictures on the bookcase: Black and white head shot of Mrs. McBreen as a slick looking young nurse.... another of her in full uniform, a nice figure, the kind a crooner in the early forties had in mind when he sang "You'd be so nice to come home to." Also a photo of what I assumed was Mr. McBreen, a fine looking young Irishman, like a combination of the young Fred MacMurray and the young Patrick O'Brien. Strong jawed, self-assured. The leader of the band. I stepped back from the bookcase and looked at another picture of him over the mantle. And then another within a cluster of pictures on the wall, this one a wedding picture with his bride.

The former bride now sat at the gloomy dining room table, her head bent, looking carefully at a list of things to do before moving to a retirement home. She was already sweating at the start of what was supposed to become a hot day.

Love always ends badly, doesn't it? No matter how much in love you are. No matter that you survived the war, went to work every day, never cheated on one another, gave the kids three squares and clean clothes every day, made love a lot or only a little, no matter what, it ends badly. One of you goes first and the other must watch with heart in throat. For the dying one, it must be like being dumped on a garbage scow and towed away, while keeping eye contact with the loved one, his one true love, his girlfriend, lover, wife, friend...partner. Share and share alike until this horrible reminder comes that we all are all separate. And she, the other, must watch her own heart's love melt and blacken and turn inward like a plastic clock consumed by fire, deteriorate, suffer, enter the grimacing world of pain, and finally, succumb. And the survivor, usually the woman: in time, her own health runs down. The kids live out of town. All the friends of their generation have also run down. They must live out the rest of their love affair alone, in sadness, becoming just a little weaker, mentally, physically, spiritually, every day. A few of them remarry and gain the illusion that they've stepped out of line, but even then, the story's always the same.

I looked at the picture of Mrs. McBreen in her wedding dress and thought, all at once: I need to leave Diane, my on and off girlfriend of the past year. I do not want to be incontinent and toothless around her, I do not trust her to give me my pain pill on time when liver cancer doubles me over, I hope tonight when Canace comes to the shop to get her poetry book she'll let me kiss her and then we'll stumble blindly forward, together, after that.

Christ, I said to myself, wake the hell up and stick to your job. There's nothing worse than having a mopey Irishman mumbling his pagan rosary on your books and pictures.

"Mrs. Mc Breen," I say, heading toward the dining room table, "I'm sorry, but there are only two books I can use. I'll pay you thirty five dollars for them."

She looked up from her list and said, "Well, that's better than nothing. I'll take it."

I felt a bit guilty for not offering to be more helpful with her problem, so without being asked I explained. There are collectors' books and readers' books and the money is in the collectors' books and that's what we sell because we run a small shop and don't have a lot of storage space. I gave Mrs. Mc Breen the phone number for Springhouse Books, the giant Internet search service we cooperate with. Mrs. Mc Breen was glad for the number and wrote it down.

I sat at the dining room table to write the check for the books and, since I'd only been there fifteen minutes and could afford a little more time, I stayed seated and asked Mrs. McBreen some questions about herself. I like to talk to most older people. Most of them, even if they seem ordinary to the eye, have led interesting lives. I've met combat pilots, infantry commanders, submarine officers, sports celebrities, company founders, FBI agents, a man who survived a famous hotel fire, another who'd been shot three times in the head and got up and walked ten miles to get help, a man who swam the Hellespont, and a woman who said she had sixteen offers of marriage in five years. Older people also know things you'd have to trade your life away for to know. What it's like to work for Schmidt's Brewery or the Tasty Baking Company for forty years, what it's like to raise a Downs Syndrome child, or have your sister murdered by her motorcycle club husband, or know what the switchover was like when the transportation company got new subway cars after you'd been riding the same old ones for thirty years. Or be a nurse, like Mrs. McBreen.

And have your husband commit suicide while the four kids were still young.

"He was...'Bipolar's' what they'd call it today," she told me across the table.

I said, "You can't see it in his face, not from those pictures in the other room."

"No. When he was up, he was really outgoing. People liked him. That's why they were all surprised." She got up to go toward the picture cluster on the wall and I followed.

I took a chance and asked: "How many good years did you have?"

I thought she'd need to think a moment before answering a question like that, but she must have reckoned the answer for her self a long time ago.

"Three," she said. No hesitation.

Then, as if she knew what my next question would be, added, "We were together for twelve. Then he killed himself."

"You were still a young woman." I pictured the panties and bra and dress on the line outside, blowing in the backyard breeze.

"Yes I was, with four young children to support. Shift work. It wasn't easy." She leaned in a little closer to the pictures. "But," here she turned and looked at me, and with a determined quaver said, "I loved my job. Outside of the kids, it was all I had."

We went back to the dining room table and talked some more. She grew up near the coal region upstate, came down here, met McBreen, such a handsome, outgoing guy. She felt a tender spot for him. There was something about him. He was adopted. He'd been in a Catholic orphanage, but was abused there, and they took him out and adopted him.

"The poor man," I said, "Poor you, so young, only three good years."

"The poor children," she said, "they never had the normal life they deserved. It was hardest on them."

There was a small silence.

Then she said, in that funny, mock-dramatic Irish way, "So that's my story and I'm sticking to it."

After that, it was either become lifetime, call-every-day friends, or it was time to go. It was only 10:40 in the morning and the place would stay dark all day unless the grandkids came over. I saw a wicker basket filled with little trucks and other toys. I was going back to work. She'd go on with her chores in that stuffed little house until she moved to the retirement home she and her daughter, who was helping her, were looking for. Disposing of the books was but one step along the way.

I went into the sunroom to get the two books I'd paid for and took another look at the picture of her and McBreen and then at McBreen alone. I'd wondered, when she tightened up her eyes and said, "I loved my job" with such emphasis what kind of nurse she'd been. I could have understood either way, hard or soft, because there was ample reason for both.

Then I noticed that McBreen's pictures were all in semi profile. A good profile it was, too, but none of them looked right at you so you could read him head on, all looking toward the future, the bright path that the elegance of his suit and strong chin and noble forehead implied he'd lead them down.

You never know, do you, what you're going to get as a go-with when you lie down beside another human being?

I shook hands with Mrs. McBreen and wished her well, which I really did, and headed back to the shop where I'd be killing time until I saw the poetry lady at five tonight. I was glad she'd said she and her husband were estranged. Her husband shouldn't have answered the phone she said. He'd merely stopped by for his old tennis racket. That's what she said, anyway.

It is almost too corny to mention, but I'll tell you anyway, because it really did happen, but out in the alley where I'd parked my car, where they collect the trash, there was a prayer card lying beside the can. I picked it up. "A Prayer For the Needy," it said. Typical nonsense, I thought. And though I wanted to trash it, I felt it would be too deliberately, dramatically, apostatic to walk twenty yards out of my way just to put it in the only trash can I saw, so I put it in my pocket to throw away later.

As I drove home, I felt a trickle of concern that if I met my fate before I could throw it away, I might be misjudged by an ambulance driver, or nurse, or policeman, or doctor, or worse, a priest, as a believer.

Chapter 5
INTO HEAVEN WITH CHAD AND BILLY

Chadford Pierce—"Chad"—called. He's an antiques dealer who gives us leads on books sometimes. Chad wanted me to leave right away to get in his van and go "see a guy" ("see a guy" deals are always weird, always warped, always done sideways) who had inherited "a whole bunch" of books from his father. The books were "really old" (They always are, supposedly, but so what? It doesn't matter, books aren't valued by their age) And such books are always described as a "collection" made by someone who "really loved old books." Those words are more often than not a tipoff that what you're about to see is worthless.

No customers had been in the shop in the past half hour and I was a little bored, so I told him to give me five minutes and I called Malachy. His daughter answered. I expressed my sympathies, always an awkward moment when you don't know a person well, and then she put Malachy on. I explained the situation and he said that since it was near closing time and it sounded vaguely promising, I should close up early and go with Chad. Fine with me.

Chad and I got in his van at 4:30 and started driving. He asked if I'd brought cash. No, I said, but I've got a signed blank check from the boss. Chad waved an envelope at me and reached to put it under his floor mat. He said, "This guy wants cash."

Carrying cash is not a good idea in the resale business. Every once in a while someone with a rep for cash payment gets a call, goes to a fake address, and is robbed, beaten, or killed. I asked Chad three times on the way to the place what the story was on the books and each answer made less sense, so I stopped asking and we just talked about the NBA playoffs and sports in general the rest of the way.

We drove into a block-long blue-collar town an hour from Chestnut Hill, turned right at such-and-such taproom, and went into its parking lot.

"What's the story on this?" I said.

"He wants to meet us in here."

What I thought was going to be a stinky deal just got stinkier. We went into the small, dim bar. It had a restaurant behind it, but they only only served dinner, so the place was empty except for one skinny, old, midday boozer wearing a security-guard shirt. Chad and I went and stood at the bar. The bartender asked if he could help us. "Yeah," Chad said, " We're supposed to meet a guy named Billy Hoffman here. You know him?"

"Sure, I know him. He ain't here, but if he said he'd meet you here, he'll be here." I love doing business with guys who have upstanding reputations for reliability in a local taproom. "Can I get you something?" he asked.

Chad had a Michelob Lite. I had a Rolling Rock, having learned from experience not to ask for imported beer in a small town bar.

Fifteen minutes went by. I was getting impatient. Straight up, regular business doesn't get done this way and Chad had a couple of thousand in cash out in the car. I told Chad that if the guy didn't show up in fifteen minutes we ought to leave. He was on his second beer by then and starting to take the rest of the day off. Great work ethic, that Chad, but it was his lead, so I had no say.

Quite a while later, in Chad-beer-years, what had to be Billy came walking in, not looking very much like the rich scion of a rich daddy book collector, as Chad had described him. He was about thirty-five, tall and slim, with pale, almost white hair that was considerably thinned out. He had probably been a good-looking kid before he got cadaverous around the cheeks and eyes.

I took him for a doper and, as he was about to demonstrate, a pretty fair boozer. He wore a straw snap-brim hat, a western-style fringed vest over a black Statler Brothers concert T-shirt, and white Docksiders. What got me most were the amateurish tattoos on his arms and the backs of his fingers, because I always figure those for prison work. I smelled a scam coming on, and my suspicions weren't relieved when he referred later to his having "been away" for a while.

Well, of course, when old friends meet, what is there to do but have a beer or two? I nursed my original Rolling Rock, but Chad and Billy had to have a nice-to-meet-cha beer, then a how-ya-been beer, and were about to have a Sixers-LA-playoff beer when I cut in and started asking about the books. Spoilsport. Billy and Chad tried glaring at me with beery contempt for being so earthbound, but eventually Billy started talking about the "collection" his bookish father had built.

The more he talked the more he resembled a weepy anus. This was not going to be a good deal and I was just about convinced we should leave. Sometimes, however, great books turn up in unlikely places. I've seen some spectacular libraries in row homes, or dilapidated barns, so I still had a shred of hope that kept me from walking outside and sticking out my thumb to hitch a ride back to Chestnut Hill.

Billy and Chad were finding that the beer went down easier if a shot of Corby's eased the way. I was getting pissed. I pushed Billy for more details, and he gave me some, but he'd started looking at me with those narrowed, measuring, resentful eyes boozers get when a downer tries to share the marquee with their fun. What he said was, his father had built a book collection—only old books, great books, really great stuff, man. And lots of them. Thousands of them, man. And he, Billy, had inherited them all, but he didn't read that much...yet...and he had nowhere to store them because the building where his father stored them had been sold and he had to get them out of there. That was his problem, man, that's why he called us, man.

Another Michelob. Another Corby's. Another small detail: This was Tuesday, all the books had to be out of there by Friday. Then he trotted out some garbled horseshit about disputations and legal claims and counter-claims and that's why we had to get moving on this, man.

6:30 p.m. I don't think I'll be making an offer to buy those books, but I'm curious to see them. If they're great books, I could put up with a whole lot of BS for the sake of purchasing them.

I get the two of them on their feet. We all better go see those books, Billy, man, time's a wastin'. Won't be much light left in the day to see the books if we don't get moving.

One more shot, a last swallow of beer and Billy was suddenly out the door and gesturing we should follow him. We went through the back of the parking lot. Billy ducked through a small gap in a big hedge and we followed. We went down an alley, through another hedge, into a narrower alley between two old brick buildings. We came to a wooden door, which Billy opened, revealing an enclosed metal staircase. We went up the steps.

"This is my old man's building," our tour guide says. The door's locked. He jiggles, pushes, pulls. Pulling works a little. The door is loose in its jamb. He and Chad pull together and create a one inch gap. I resist asking why Billy doesn't use his key. While they confab, I look through the glass and see a huge empty office space, partitions between individual spaces knocked askew, directories of various kinds lying on the floors. An abandoned business.

We all go back down stairs. Billy stands with one foot on the first step, rubs his chin for a minute, tucks in his lower lip, takes off his hat, wipes his brow, picks up something I can't see and turns to Chad, says, "Go for the gold, right?" Chad says, "I didn't come this far to play with myself."

"That's it then," and back up the stairs we go. I feel like the singer in the "Please Mister Custer, ah don' wanna go" song, but I bring up the rear. Billy has a three-foot piece of metal pipe. He and Chad work it into the gap and then go crazy working it back and forth, their faces red with effort, the cords in their necks strained. And then, snap, crackle, pop—the door jumps off its hinges and we are in.

We went around a corner, another corner, through an aisle, around yet another corner, and came to a large open area lined with metal office-style bookcases. The Old Man's Library. Eldorado. Floor to ceiling, eight shelves to a case, at least forty linear feet of them, the books double and triple stacked. Tah dah! Go for the gold. Even from twenty-five feet away, however, I knew at a glance they were junk. Oh, yes, definitely, a bookman can judge books by their covers.

Most of what I was looking at were twentieth-century cloth-covered books, the majority of them popular fiction. They had the faded, dirty, moldy, seedy, scuffed, warped, water-damaged look of books you'd find in an old bookbarn in Maine where the seller had no idea what a desirable book was, but reckoned that anything old could price out at ten cents per year of age. Cloth books of this type were published by the millions and usually have no value, some exception being made for books with collectible dust jackets, which none of these books had. They were the kind of old-fashioned looking books a shrewd, compulsive, hoarder who didn't know any better would buy at flea markets and church sales for ten cents or a quarter because he was convinced they were worth more than what the fools were charging.

Billy's father could never have read all this drivel. They'd obviously been bought as an investment. "All yours son, they'll be worth a lot of money someday." And behind the shrewdness, probably, some sad 'Rosebud'-type link stretched back to a book the old man had seen or owned once as a youth. The Eternal Hunger. Great or small, collecting feeds on the hunger to regain something lost. I think it's the desire to adopt an orphaned self.

"These are my dad's books, man." Billy was moist-eyed. In the bar, he called him his "old man," but here in the shrine, it was "Dad." I wasn't in the mood for genuflecting, or faking my way through the high-wire balancing act you need to do when guys like Billy get drunk, I just wanted out of there. I did not want to pretend to be giving these mold-gatherers the reverence needed to redeem Billy's messed-up life. I did not want to touch my chin, say hmmm, and wipe my brow, and get out pencil and paper, do the whole charade, and then tell him how great his legacy was, but not quite what I could use. Find me a drunk that'll give you the time of day, who'll listen to your story.

Especially now. His eyes had taken on that trick appearance weepy drinkers get, like those lightly corrugated plastics with a picture inside that you hold in your hand. Standing at this angle, Billy was a devoted son, an inheritor revealing what had been behind door number two all his life. And seen from this other angle, he was a shifty jerk about to go chameleon on me and get offended and nasty if I didn't tell him how great this stuff was.

"Take your time, man. Great stuff, huh?"

"Sure are a lot of them," I said, pretending to be too overwhelmed by the volume to comment on their greatness.

'Yeah, well, he was out there, man. All the time. He was there before the dealers even. Everywhere. Perkiomenville, Lahaska, 309 when they had it, you name it. All yours man. What I want's fifteen hundred, that's all, that's like twenty-five cents a book or something. Look it over, tell me what you think."

"He's the bookman," Chad said, "What else you got?"

"I'll show you," Billy said, as though words could not begin to describe hidden treasures unknown, and he wandered off through the maze of partitions, Chad following him. I started examining the books, hoping there was a pony somewhere in the midst of all this happy horseshit and that a deal was possible. I started pulling the first rank of books out and looking at the ones behind them. In dismay, I saw some of the shelves were triple-stacked. I looked at my watch. Nearly seven. I wanted out of there.

Billy was back, his arm hooked through the front end of a 10-foot aluminum ladder, Chad holding up the rear. Billy looked up at the four-by-three ceiling tiles as he reversed, came forward, moved to the side, then stopped, Chad meanwhile getting the whiplash end of things because he didn't set the ladder down until Billy made that final zig. Just like The Three Stooges. Billy started opening the ladder, which was the most rickety ladder I'd ever seen, a geezer, with twists and creases bent into the bracing pieces and a broken bottom step.

Everything then began to speed up. Billy scrambled up the ladder and pushed up a tile. Nope. Back down. Moved the ladder, fast, in a hurry, tried again, nope. Got it the third time. Tried to toss the tile like a frisbee but it just hit the partition next to him and crumbled, pieces falling on Chad.

"Whoa," Chad says.

"No whoa, man, we're going to heaven." Billy's head and neck, to the shoulders, disappeared and I could see him only from the chest down atop the woozy stepladder. He had pushed open a trap-door six inches above the false ceiling and then, with a flex of the knees and a jump that made the ladder fall, he sprang up into the crawl space or attic or whatever was up there. Chad said, "Gimme a hand with this," and he reset the ladder like this was Iwo Jima. We could hear Billy thunking around up there, tossing heavy things. I steadied the ladder for Chad and he too went up and out of sight. They were talking loudly, excitedly, up there, but the ceiling muted their words.

I was curious, but no way. I've worked construction work and done enough other things involving ladders to have a deep and abiding respect for their ability to transform able-bodied men into quadriplegics. And work with two guys that'd been drinking? I'll stay grounded and light flares for the medivacs, thank you. But then, Chad said, "You gotta come up here, Brian, there's books, there's magazines, there's old calendar pictures, diaries, you name it, all kinds of shit."

"Shit," I believed, but curiosity overcame me, so I squared the shaky ladder as best I could and ascended it slowly. When I got up high enough, I grabbed the ceiling struts with both hands and then stood on the top step and looked in on the upstairs neighbors. By the stark light of two bare, hundred-watt bulbs Chad and Billy were pulling things aside, looking in boxes, and holding things up to the light, not caring that they were stepping on the very ancient-looking, plastered lath between the joists up there.

"C'mon up, man," Chad said. There was more print-ed material than anything else up there, so he needed me to interpret its worth. He obviously thought it had value, because he had a big smile on his face and was holding stuff up like a kid turned loose in toyland.

By raising both arms and standing on tiptoe, my armpits were even with the ceiling. I flexed my toes and jumped while pulling myself up.The ladder toppled side-ways before I got lift and I lost my grip. As I fell, I scraped my side painfully on the metal trapdoor frame. I landed on the spread ladder, scraping my shins and one ankle. My chest was raw and oozing where I'd hit, and my legs were scraped, but I didn't break anything or get wacked in the balls I was hoping so much to use again sometime.

On my second try, the ladder held and I ascended into wonderland. Voilá! More junk. As far as the eye could see. I walked the joists and examined every tied-up bun-dle. Family Circle Magazine from the 1970s. Real-estate company calendars with reproductions of Currier and Ives pictures. Boxes of Styrofoam drinking cups. Rip, rip: an-other bundle opened, newspaper and magazine clippings and pictures of movie stars. Rip, rip again: newspapers–Kennedy assassination, Moon Walk, Philadelphia Bulle-tin's Last Issue. Same old, same old, saved in nearly every attic or closet I've been into.

Billy was saying, "So, it's a long way down to haul all this stuff out, so I figured you guys could make a chute or something and zip this stuff down to your truck or some-thing."

Chad: "That's a possibility. Definitely."

"Just so it's all out of here by Friday, is all. We can't get in here after that."

I said I'd seen enough to get a good idea, the big picture, you know, and then climbed down, no mishaps, and waited for them. Chad descended holding some collectible toy soldiers and an old Stieff teddy bear, happy to return to Earth and obviously looking forward to his next orbit. Billy said to me, "We got a deal here, pardner?"

I needed a second to think of how I should say I didn't want any part of him or his father's books. What I wanted to say was: If this book collection had been the purpose of the old man's existence, his crowning achievement, what he'd worked and pushed toward all his life, what had made his life worth living, what he'd hoped to point towards on his deathbed and say, "It was all worthwhile, look what I've done," the old man had wasted his time. There wasn't a speck of taste or emotion there, and I don't mean that in a snobbish way. I mean that there was no obvious love of books or reverence for the printed word. The whole assemblage reeked of one principle: I'm buying this book because I'm smarter than the guy who sold it to me and I know its worth better than he does. But Billy's old man was wrong.

Billy had developed that red-rimmed, drying-out look some guys get as they enter the touchy-sneaky phase of their drinking bouts, so I tried being diplomatic and said, "Your father put together quite a bunch of books here, but they're not what we sell."

"You don't think they're good enough?"

I wanted to knock him on his ass then and there. I'm getting to the point in life where I'm tired of tiptoeing around people who walk as flat and loud as they please.

"Yeah, they're good books, they're just not what we sell." Chad's looking ready to interrupt. To an antiques dealer, old is old, and old usually means money.

Billy said, "Oh, so you don't sell good books?" Caught me out in a logic trap.

I said, "Here's how I see it, just one man's opinion, okay? These books are about ninety-five percent fiction, stories and such, that were popular in their day, but nowadays they're hard to sell unless you have the customers for them. We just don't have the customers for them. You need a guy who handles this kind of stuff." Try Mars.

He was quiet for a few seconds before he said, "So, what are they worth to you?" He was taking me for a hard bargainer. That made it tougher, because now that he'd cracked, he was going to be even more sensitive to a slight.

"I really couldn't say. I just don't think we can handle them the right way, you know what I mean?"

'Okay, okay, I hear you, man, but I gotta move on this stuff. Five hundred bucks, take em all."

"Just can't do it. And I don't want to waste any more of your time, so we'd best be getting back."

I nodded to Chad that I wanted to go. I could tell he wanted to make a deal, but wanted to talk to me first, to see what kind of rocks I had in my head.

"Fuck it, man," Billy said, "take the whole god-dammed thing for three hundred bucks, the attic, the books, whatever you find." There was hurt and anger in his eyes then.

"It's not the money, this isn't about money," I said. His desperation made me wonder if, at that moment, Billy and Chad, and I by complicity, could be charged with Breaking and Entering, Burglary, Larceny, and Conspiracy, to name a few likely charges. Maybe there was no 'Billy's dad' here. Maybe these books belonged to Billy's former boss, or the guy Billy used to deliver pizzas to, or some other person from whom Billy's right of inheritance was equally tenuous.

Looking at Chad, Billy said, "Come on, you guys, let's go talk it over. Get a beer. Figure something out."

Chad said, "Sounds good to me."

We all went back through the blasted door, down the iron staircase, up the alley through the holes in the bushes and wound up back in the parking lot outside the tavern. Along the way, I'd managed under my breath to convince Chad that we had to go and I should drive. He had all that cash in the car and it was now dark and we were in a dimly-lit parking lot behind a strange bar in a neighborhood we'd never been to before. We weren't doing a deal today. He grumbled, but gave me the keys.

Billy was waiting for us in the parking lot. I told him we had something we had to get from the van. I opened the passenger door of the van for Chad and he climbed in. I went around and climbed in behind the wheel and started the engine.

Billy got a look on his face I enjoyed putting there. It was a look of surprise that what he thought he was watching on television was really happening. The two guys he'd just spent all that time with had just got in their van and were leaving. Without cinching the deal.

"Wait a minute, you guys. What about that beer?"

I said, "Later on that. Thanks anyway. We gotta get back. But, tell you what: I'm going to tell another dealer I know about these books. I'm pretty sure he'll want them."

I gave him the business card of Croesus Books, a bookshop in New Jersey whose card I had. They only handle the rarest of the rare, and Billy fit that description. "Here's his number."

He was still sputtering about the beer as I drove Chad's van out of the parking lot. Chad had paid Billy a hundred bucks cash for the toy soldiers and another hundred for the Stieff bear. He seemed happy, and he was free to go back. Just then, I wanted nothing to do with either of them. My scrapes had stopped oozing and started to dry my shirt to my skin. I'd had enough trouble for one day, even though I'd probably hurt Billy more than he'd hurt me.

Chapter 6
TRAPPED IN A
BOOKSHOP

In which the narrator is now the owner and proprietor of an Old & Rare bookshop in Chestnut Hill, Philadelphia. "It must be so great to sit around and read all those wonderful books every day."

I'll ignore the fact that those who say such things don't usually sully their love with money. They just poke their heads in the doorway, sigh their envy, and then return to gleaning the FREE books on the doorstep.

Those are books I've put out to honor The Diggers and to propitiate the gods who might otherwise send stick-up artists in their place.

My bookshop is open predictably only on Fridays and Saturdays, 11-4. On those days, I go in early and stay late in order to do my daily quota of writing. I put up the "Closed" sign and turn out all the lights except the one in the back room where I'm working. From outside, the shop looks uninhabited.

On a Friday night a few weeks ago, after I closed the shop, I finished my first piece for The Chestnut Hill Notebook (the first "Enemies of Reading: Waiting Room TV's"). I hadn't paid attention to the time and didn't notice night had fallen until I turned off the lights in the back room. I paused to let my eyes adjust before walking through the dark shop. The eternal piles of books on the floor shift as sneakily as sand dunes and could easily trip me so I'd fall and hit my head on the corner of a piece of furniture and get knocked out and bleed to death like William Holden.

In that second's pause, I saw that someone was on the doorstep, going through the FREE books outside. Looked like a man. What to do, what to do?

I hate this scenario. Some poor guy or gal is going through the books in the dark, looking for something to read, or hoping to find the Rosebud book of their youth, and suddenly, and without warning, I've soundlessly crept up to the door and: Thrown The Lights On!

Aha, caught you!

Not the feeling I'm trying to promote. In fact I am promoting nothing. I simply cannot throw away a book and I'm lucky enough to have a doorstep and a handmade sign that says FREE.

If I do snap on the lights, the night browsers look up like wildlife at a midnight salt lick. That's when my drab life gets interesting, because I don't know what kind of eyes are going to be blinking back at me from the book pile.

If I've disturbed a mouse, then I feel as sorry as Robert Burns when he turned up a mouse nest with his plough:

I'm truly sorry Man's dominion
Has broken Nature's social union
An' justifies that ill opinion
Which makes thee startle

At me, thy poor, earth-born companion,
And fellow-mortal.

But if it's a wolf, I've just shined the lights on myself. It is I who will feel like running away, "a panic in my breastie."

No brainer, right? Turn the lights on, I've either embarrassed some book lover, or I've exposed myself to one of the things that could bump me in the night.

I decide to wait it out in the darkness of the shop. That sounds stupid, doesn't it? Gutless. I don't mind. What's another few minutes if it's linked to life extension? But, I was also tired, hungry, and anxious to leave and go see my girlfriend. I kept coming through the shop and was nearing the door, where the light switch is, when I heard him talking. Something in the tone of his voice stopped me. He sounded angry.

There's no other exit from the shop than the front door. I'd wait a minute for him to leave. I walked around to my desk near the window, figuring to key in a VISA number from an Internet sale on my credit card machine, a task I could do using the light that came in the window from the street.

Whoever was outside had propped a racing bike against the doorway and was wearing a bicycle helmet. He also had a long, unkempt beard. The frame of the doorway kept me from seeing more. Blocked him from seeing me. He kept up a steady stream of conversation, not angry anymore. Silly me, I thought, he's on his cell phone. Oh well. He'll be done browsing and talking and ride off in a minute.

Sort of hiding in the dark, no longer in fear, but feeling I'd look strange prowling around in my own shop in the dark, I hunched over the desk and entered the card numbers in the machine. Click, click, click, and "Enter." The printer kicked in, making what sounded under the circumstances like an enormous racket.

"Who's there?" the voice from the doorstep demanded.

I froze.

"Mumble, mumble, mumble, angry mumble," I heard. I saw he didn't have a cell phone. He'd been talking to himself.

Oh my, I've angered the gods, I thought. Oh how I wish I had a back door. The streets were deserted. I could see the man pressing his face against the glass of the door, trying to see in.

"There's a time to live and a time to die," he roared.

Oh shit.

I eased to the back of the shop, taking advantage of the angled shadows, and stood in the backroom's doorway, partly shielded by a chin-high bookcase. I could see him, but he couldn't see me.

He began walking back and forth across the front of the store, like a zoo animal, never taking his eyes off the interior of the shop. He seemed angry. Something that threatened him was lurking inside this place. Something was watching him. Only, unlike myself, he was hunting for whatever he felt had been stalking him.

I never felt so much in my life like a small animal, down in a hole, listening to the heavy sniffing up above, waiting for the sounds of the earth being pawed away.

He put his face against the glass (glass!—an eighth of an inch), cupping his hands like blinders around his eyes so he could see inside better.

"There's a time to live and a time to die," he said again, laughing at the wonderful, hideous truth of his declaration.

Whose time though? His, because he was wiling to risk attacking his enemy? Or mine, because I'd put out milk and cookies for the kittens and managed to attract a golem?

I felt my cell phone in my pocket. Two questions: How much time do I give this drama before I seek help? Who do I call?

The time element? Well, if he doesn't try to break in, I'll wait him out. He hasn't seen me, I'm guessing, because he hasn't said anything like,

"I see you."

Or, "Come out of there, you varmint."

He merely suspects I'm here. I'm counting on him being the kind of guy who suspects lots of things that aren't there. And even though he is, technically, right this time, I'm hoping he says, "Silly me," and gives up. I'll give it fifteen minutes, maybe a half hour.

But if I'm wrong. If the siege goes on "too long," or he tries to break in, I'll call for help. At one point, the local police officer gave me his patrol bike cell phone number, but that's on a piece of paper right near where my free-book patron is mumbling with his face against the window. So I guess it's 911. But what do I say? I start working on the wording of my cry for help. These 911 tapes get played on the news. As a bookman, I have a certain obligation to provide a coherent, perhaps even eloquent, sound bite for TV.

And then...I'm not sure, but I think I haven't heard him for a...second? a minute? And I lean out beyond the bookcase, looking at the front door. I don't see him. He may be laying a trap. I wait a little longer and then walk stealthily forward. I don't see the bike in the doorway.

In a little while, still in the dark, I open the door, bracing my foot against the bottom in case I have to push it shut against resistance. Nothing. I step partly out and look up the block. Deserted. Far up the street, passing OMC Church, a man is walking a bicycle. Away from me.

I lock the door and walk down the alley to my car. I get in, lock the doors and start the car. As I pull away, I am feeling like Wally Shawn at the end of *My Dinner With Andre*: I'm grateful to be going over to the poetry lady's house tonight. Things have been going well between us. We'll eat dinner together and probably make love and read in bed together for a while. I like the book I'm reading now. Tomorrow I'll get up early and go in to write and I'll open the shop again at 11 a.m. and hope to sell some books. And after work I'll write again, but I'll be careful about the time and try to leave before it gets dark.

Only, Wally Shawn, riding a cab home, looking out at the streets of New York at night, was really looking forward to telling his girlfriend, Debbie, all about the time he spent with Andre. I don't think I want to tell my story tonight. It will make it seem too real. I'll hold off for a while.

In the meanwhile, I feel in my heart a version of what I call "The Merchant's Prayer": "Thank You Dear Lord for not sending anyone to rob, shoot, or stab me simply because I run a public business in the city. Especially one where the perp is dumb enough to think there's money to be had."

Amen.

But Wait—THE SEQUEL...

Seldom is a man so blessed: The next day, Saturday, near closing time, I opened the door and stepped outside for some air. In the same instant a tall, rangy, bearded guy dressed as "a street person" walked up and said,

"Hi, any new ones today?"

Same beard shape and body build. No bike or helmet.

"Yeah, I put out some good ones today," I said.

"Man, I couldn't believe my good luck last night," he said, "to actually find a Wallace Stevens poetry book. With the complete poems. Amazing, man."

He was missing a few display teeth and his eyelids had drawn way back to enable the obvious fervor he brought to life.

"Good for you, " I said, "I was hoping someone who appreciated him would find the book."

I'd put it out for free because the lettering on the spine was faded and browsers would be unlikely to even examine such a book. "Can't read the spine—can't sell the book," we say.

"Appreciate him?" he said, starting to wind up for a speech. He had the look in his eye of a man who could and would talk at length. I felt like asking for a forensic voice sample on the line "There's a time to live and a time to die," but I didn't really need one.

"Appreciate Wallace Stevens?" He continued, "Why he grew up on Fifth Street, North Fifth Street, in Reading. I used to deliver the paper to that house. He wasn't there any more, he lived in Connecticut by then, but still it was an honor. His house is still there. That was the first famous person I ever crossed paths with, so to speak, but not the last. Then there was…"

"He was from Reading?" I said. That sounded dubious.

"Yeah, Reading. Went to Reading Public High School. Oh yeah, he was from Reading."

Well, live and learn, huh? I listened for a while. I had to come off the doorstep because he was upwind of me and the reek of stale urine from his greasy pants made me feel I was trapped in a subway tunnel. He went on and on. I was thinking, Where'd you come from, buddy?

Everybody is some mother's child. What path led this former baby boy who gathers books from my doorstep by day to being the unkempt, smelly, wild-haired, loony "street person" who looks through my shop window for his demons at night? He seemed like a lost child right now. He seemed hungry to be listened to. I felt sorry for him.

"I've got to get back to work," I said, "take it easy."

"Okay, thanks for the books. And, uh, I'm Marty by the way," offering his hand, which turned out to be bony and wet. We shook. He walked back up Bethlehem Pike, carrying his FREE book for today—Will Durant's The Story of Philosophy. Volume four, I think.

Now, if I refer to the scare he gave me and the conversation we had about Wallace Stevens, I refer to is with Canace as My Dinner With Marty.

Sequel to the sequel: Yes, I Googled Wallace Stevens: 323 North Fifth Street, Reading Pennsylvania, 1879. Reading Public High School.

Yes, I know: "Cowards die a thousand deaths." I'm still around to tell you that.

ABOUT THE AUTHOR

Hugh Gilmore owned and operated a book shop in Chestnut Hill, Philadelphia, for 12 years. The business now runs as Gilmore's Books, without a shop. He is the author of *Malcolm's Wine*, a noir crime novel set in the rare book business. He writes a weekly column called "The Enemies of Reading" for the Chestnut Hill Local newspaper and maintains a blog called **enemiesofreading.blogspot. com**. He lives in Philadelphia with his wife, the writer Janet Gilmore, and his talented son, Andrew.